nickelodeon

Dora & Diego

WHERE IS BABY JAGUAR?

by Laura Driscoll
illustrated by Tom Mangano

Ready-to-Read

Simon Spotlight/Nickelodeon
New York   London   Toronto   Sydney

This book was previously published as *Dora Helps Diego!*

Based on the TV series *Dora the Explorer*™ and *Go, Diego, Go*™ as seen on Nick Jr.™

SIMON SPOTLIGHT
An imprint of Simon & Schuster Children's Publishing Division
1230 Avenue of the Americas, New York, New York 10020
© 2007, 2011 Viacom International Inc. NICKELODEON, NICK JR., *Dora the Explorer, Go, Diego, Go!*, and all related
titles, logos, and characters are trademarks of Viacom International Inc.
All rights reserved, including the right of reproduction in whole or in part in any form.
SIMON SPOTLIGHT, READY-TO-READ, and colophon are registered trademarks of Simon & Schuster, Inc.
For information about special discounts for bulk purchases, please contact Simon & Schuster Special Sales at
1-866-506-1949 or business@simonandschuster.com.
Manufactured in the United States of America 1210 LAK
This Simon Spotlight edition 2011
2 4 6 8 10 9 7 5 3
ISBN 978-1-4424-1398-6

This book was previously published as *Dora Helps Diego!*

Hi! I am  .
DORA

, , and I

need your help!

DIEGO   BOOTS

Oh, no! is missing!
BABY JAGUAR

 cannot find him!
DIEGO

 and I
BOOTS

are helping find him.
DIEGO

Will you help too?

Great!

Help us find  !

BABY JAGUAR

Look up in that .

TREE

I see a 🐾.

TAIL

has a .

BABY JAGUAR   TAIL

Does it belong to ?

BABY JAGUAR

No.

It is a  SNAKE

getting out of the  SUN .

Where is BABY JAGUAR?

Look behind those .

FLOWERS

I see 🦶🦶.

FEET

has .

BABY JAGUAR   FEET

Do they belong to  ?

BABY JAGUAR

No.

It is  ISA

working in her . GARDEN

Where is ?

BABY JAGUAR

Look behind that trunk.
TREE

I see .
WHISKERS

 has .

BABY JAGUAR WHISKERS

Do those belong

WHISKERS

to ?

BABY JAGUAR

No.

It is , that sneaky fox.
SWIPER

Where is  ?
BABY JAGUAR

Look behind the .

SLIDE

I see .

SPOTS

 BABY JAGUAR has  SPOTS .

Do they belong to  BABY JAGUAR ?

No.

It is the scarf that belongs to .

BENNY

Will we **ever** find  ?

BABY JAGUAR

We need to go back to

the Animal Rescue Center.

We open the . DOOR

We cannot believe it!